Mel Bay Presents

CHRISTMAS SONGS

FOR HARMONICA

By Phil Duncan

CD CONTENTS

1. Jingle Bells Medley (*Jingle Bells, Jolly Old St. Nicholas, Up On The House Top, Deck the Halls, Jingle Bells* reprise) G**, [2:09]
2. O Little Town Of Bethlehem, C Chromatic, G, [3:48]
3. Angels Medley (*Angels We Have Heard On High; Angels, From The Realms Of Glory, Hark! The Herald Angels Sing, Angels We Have Heard On High* reprise), G**, [1:56]
4. O Come All Ye Faithful, It Came Upon The Midnight Clear, O Come, All Ye Faithful reprise, G**- A♭**- A**, [4:37]
5. O Christmas Tree, G**, [2:18]
6. The Birthday Of A King, C Chromatic, C, [4:08]
7. The Coventry Carol, C Chromatic, Am, [3:33]
8. Go Tell It On The Mountain, G**- A♭**, [3:42]
9. The First Noel, C*, [5:22]
10. Joy To The World with *Glory to God* from the *Messiah*, C*- D♭*, [3:02]
11. I Heard The Bells On Christmas Day (two tunes), C Chromatic, C, B♭**- E♭**, [3:45]
12. O Holy Night, G***, [3:08]
13. What Child Is This? C Chromatic, Am, [2:49]
14. Away In A Manger, Silent Night, Away In A Manger reprise, G**, [3:24]
15. Merry Christmas Medley (*We Wish You A Merry Christmas*, C*, *The Wassail Song*, C*, *We Saw Three Ships*, C*- E♭*, *We Wish You a Merry Christmas* reprise, G**- A♭**), [2:57]

Total Time: 52:12   *Standard Tuning   **Country Tuned   ***Melody Maker

Keyboard: Dan Roberts
Orchestration accompaniments recorded and arranged: Dan Roberts
Post production: Westend Recording Studios, Kansas City, KS 66103

Engineered, edited and mastered: Bart Blechele
Digital mastering: Mike Miller
Chromatic and Diatonic Harmonica: Phil Duncan

---

1 2 3 4 5 6 7 8 9 0

Visit us on the Web at http://www.melbay.com — E-mail us at email@melbay.com

Table of Musical Contents

Diatonic Harmonica

Each harmonica is designed in a certain "key". When using the harmonica in that stated "key" it is called standard or straight harmonica, such as the C harmonica is the key of C, the G harmonica is the key of G and the F harmonica is the key of F, etc. This also means that the center or "home" tone is the fourth hole of the diatonic harmonica. Each different key requires a different harmonica. You may be able to use any key harmonica in this book if you observe the numbers and arrows written below each musical line. Normally you would use the C harmonica for this book.

In playing straight harmonica, the method for blocking out unwanted tones is called "tongue blocking". Your tongue should cover and block off two or three undesired holes on the left of the harmonica mouth piece:

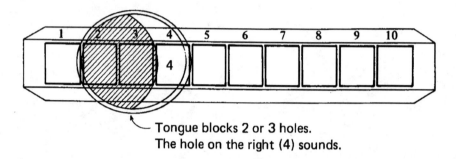

Tongue blocks 2 or 3 holes.
The hole on the right (4) sounds.

To be able to "chord" with melody, just release the tonque covered holes and a chord (3 or more tone together) will be produced.

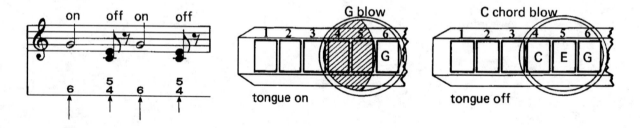

DIATONIC 10 HOLE NOTE CHART

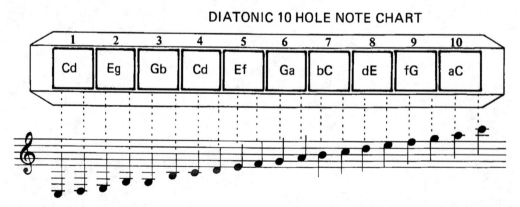

FOR FURTHER INFORMATION about the diatonic harmonica refer to: Mel Bay's DELUXE HARMONICA METHOD by Phil Duncan.

4

Chromatic Harmonica

The use of the slide button will give accurate half-step tones on the chromatic harmonica. The 12 or 16 hole chromatic harmonica have been notated in this book. A change of octaves becomes necessary for variety and ease of playing. (All octaves on the chromatic harmonica are the same, except the tones are higher or lower in pitch.)

EXAMPLE:

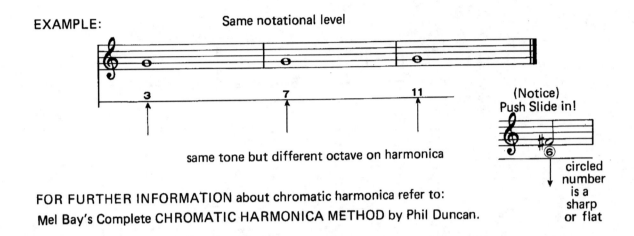

Same notational level

same tone but different octave on harmonica

(Notice)
Push Slide in!

circled
number
is a
sharp
or flat

FOR FURTHER INFORMATION about chromatic harmonica refer to:
Mel Bay's Complete CHROMATIC HARMONICA METHOD by Phil Duncan.

Cross-Harp
(Blues Harp Style)

The method for cross-harp is to cross over to hole 2 of the diatonic 10 hole harmonica and draw. This tone becomes (hole 2) the "key" center or "home" tone and changes the "key" in which the harmonica plays. Therefore, C harp plays cross-harp (blues harp) in the key of G. (G is the draw tone in hole 2) F harp plays cross-harp in the key of C. (C is a draw tone in hole 2 of the F harp) If the music is in the key of C use the F harmonica. The cross-harp technique allows for half step tones not normally played on the diatonic harmonica. All draw tones should begin below the pitch: then rise quickly to pitch level.

To achieve the half steps, a blues technique called bending is used.
Notational information:

③ = half step down   ③ = whole step down   ▽③ = whole step and a half

Octave changes need to take place for ease of playing. The numbers will dictate the changes:

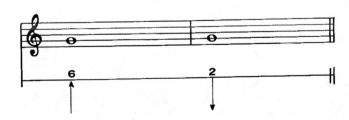

Notes in paranthesis are subsitute notes:

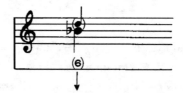

LIP BLOCKING is used to produce the single tone. This allows for greater pressure on the harmonica reeds. The harmonica player simply purses his lips so that only one sound can be made.

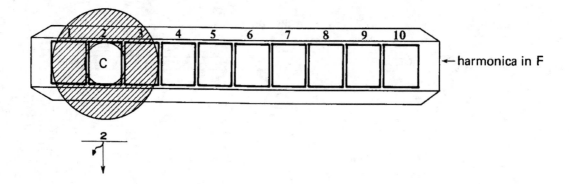

←harmonica in F

FILLS: added notes that are optional tones to be played at the end of phrases or breaks in the music. They can be added to the melody or just used as fill between the vocals.

Cross-harp can play these added notes:

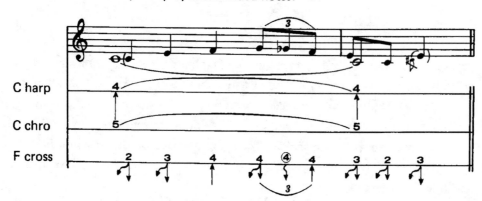

FOR FURTHER INFORMATION about cross-harp refer to: BLUES HARP for Diatonic and Chromatic Harmonica by Phil Duncan

6

General Information

1. BLOW   DRAW

2. Top arrow is the rule:

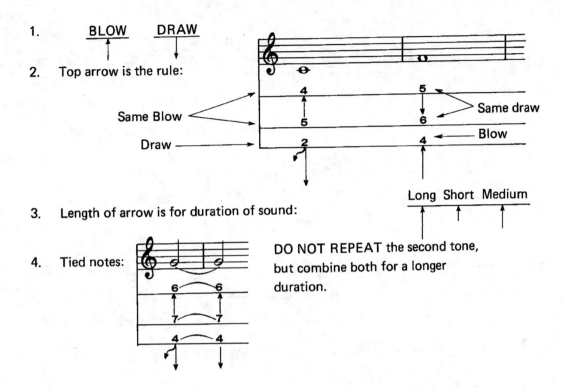

    Same Blow

    Draw

    Same draw

    Blow

    Long Short Medium

3. Length of arrow is for duration of sound:

4. Tied notes:

    DO NOT REPEAT the second tone,
    but combine both for a longer
    duration.

C harmonica, Diatonic

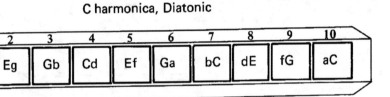

F cross - Harp

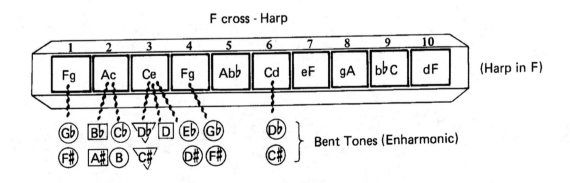

(Harp in F)

Bent Tones (Enharmonic)

C harmonica, Chromatic

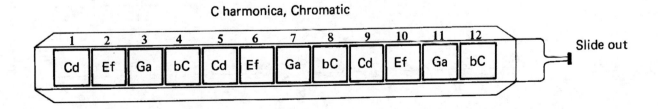

Slide out

Amen

Spiritual

8

Angels, From The Realms Of Glory

Henry Smart 1867

J. Montgomery, 1810

Angels We Have Heard On High

Away In A Manger

German

Birthday Of A King

W.H. Neidlinger

The Coventry Carol

Robert Coo, 1534

English Melody 1891

* Use of the G harp for A minor (hole 4, draw, in "center" tone)" minor" cross Begins in draw hole 4 (3rd position).
** Picardy Third (raise C third tone) * Use of D harp, hole 3, draw.
　　　　　　　　(in a minor key.)

Bring A Torch, Jeannette, Isabella

French

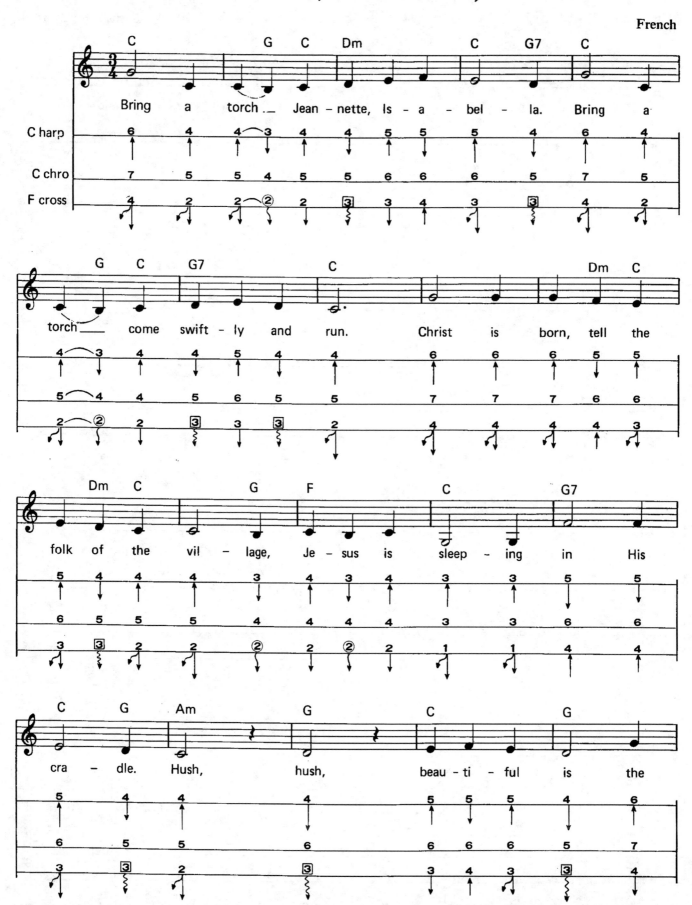

14

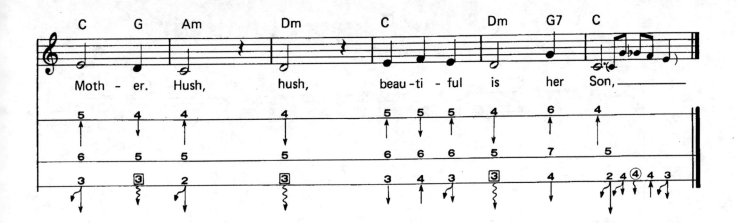

While Shepherds Watched Their Flocks By Night

G.F. Handel

* C harmonica is used for proper pitch level.

Dance Of The Sugar-Plum Fairy

P.I Tchaikovsky

* G minor-cross (3rd position) uses G harp with the center tone in hole 4, draw.

Deck The Hall

Welsh Air

The First Noel

Fum, Fum, Fum

Spanish

* G minor-cross (3rd position) uses G harp.

Go Tell It On The Mountain

Spiritual

God Rest Ye Merry, Gentleman

English Carol

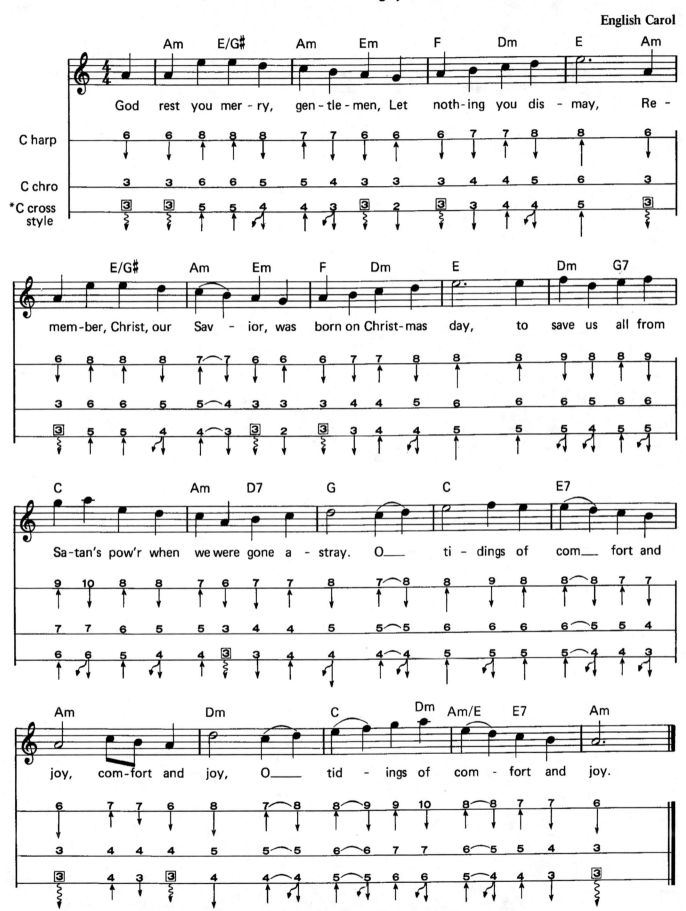

* C harp with bent tones give a "Blues style" sound (4th position).

Good Christian Men, Rejoice

German Carol

Good King Wenceslas

Hark! The Herald Angels Sing

C. Wesley

F. Mendelssohn

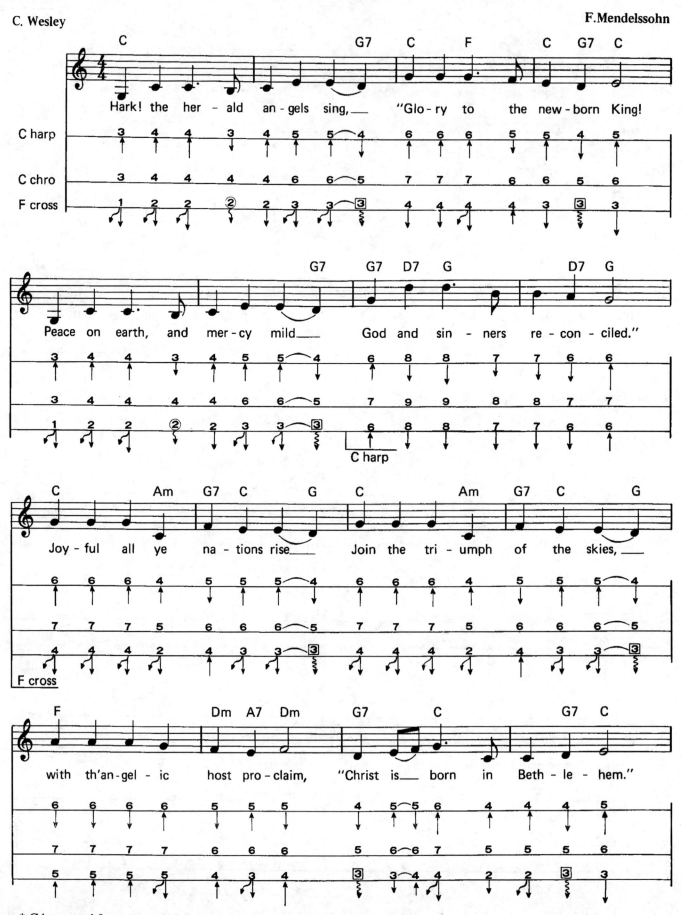

* C harp used for proper pitch level.

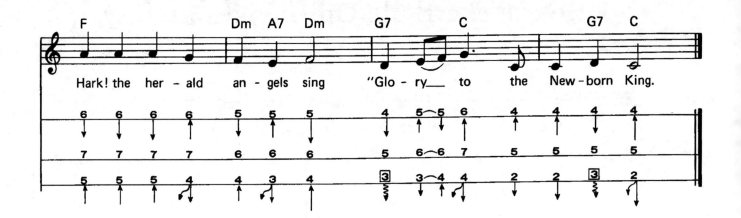

I Saw Three Ships

I Heard The Bells On Christmas Day

H.W. Longfellow

J.B. Calkin

Jolly Old Saint Nicholas

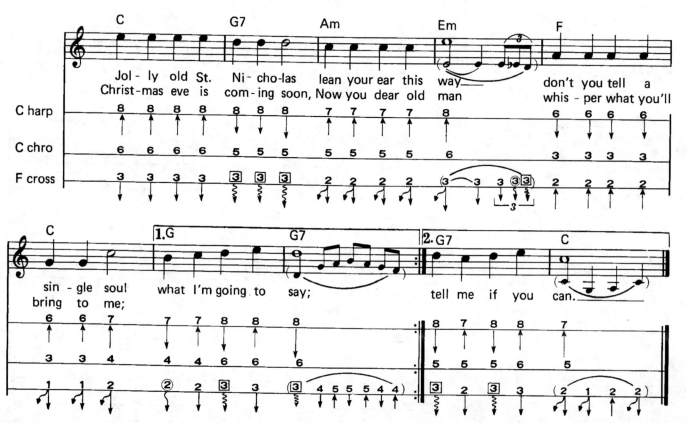

It Came Upon The Midnight Clear

Jingle Bells

F. J. Pierpont

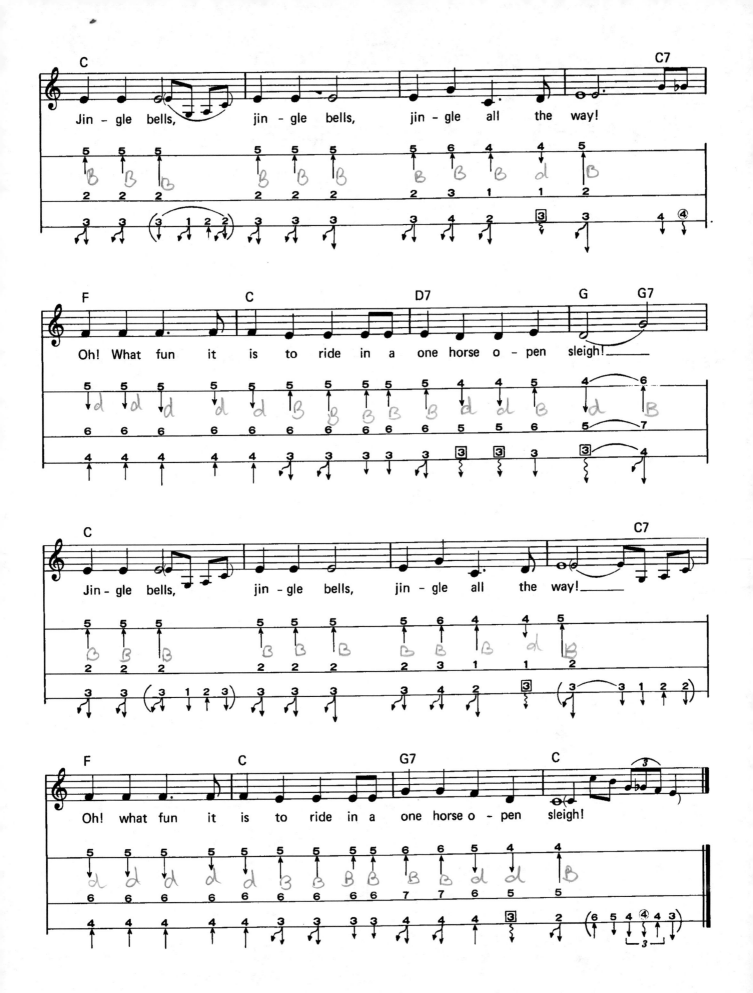

Joy To The World

G.F. Handel

Mary Had A Baby

Arr. P. Duncan

We Wish You A Merry Christmas

Old English

O Christmas Tree

German Carol

32

O Come, All Ye Faithful

J. Reading

O Holy Night

Adolphe Adam

* C harp is used for proper pitch level.

O Little Town Of Bethlehem

P. Brooks

L.H. Redner

Silent Night

F. Gruber

We Three Kings Of Orient Are

J.H. Hopkins

* G minor-cross is 4th hole draw on the G harmonica, 3rd position.

*F cross

*Key change to C from A minor

What Child Is This?

English Air

* G minor-cross, hole 4 is center tone on G harmonica, 3rd position.

40

Auld Lang Syne

Love And Joy
(Wassail Song)

Hanukah

Hebrew Folk Song

* Special toy (Top)
** Note Harp change.

Hanukah Hymn

Hebrew Hymn

Candles Of Hanukah

Hebrew

* G minor-cross uses G harmonica, draw hole 4 is the center tone, 3rd position.

Great Music at Your Fingertips

INTRODUCTION TO
caRD
creations

igloobooks

igloobooks

Published in 2015
by Igloo Books Ltd
Cottage Farm
Sywell
NN6 0BJ
www.igloobooks.com

Cover images © Thinkstock / Getty Images

LEO002 0715
2 4 6 8 10 9 7 5 3 1
ISBN 978-1-78440-285-3

Printed and manufactured in China

INTRODUCTION TO card creations

Contents

Introduction

Cards are the perfect way to express a wide variety of sentiments. From 'Happy Birthday' to 'Congratulations!', every occasion can be marked with a beautiful card.

Handmade cards add a deeper level of charm to every thoughtful sentiment; taking the time to plan and create something personal can be exceptionally rewarding for the card-maker and the receiver. Inside this book, you will find everything that you need to know to create special cards for everyone.

With step-by-step instructions to the card-making process and a wide variety of designs, this book will guide you through the materials and equipment you'll need to get started and will inspire you to create your very own designs.

With ideas for birthdays, weddings, seasonal occasions and more, there's a card for everyone in Card Creations.

Instructions

Whether you've just started card-making or you're already a seasoned crafter, it's often worth taking a look at your essentials and making sure you've got everything you're likely to need.

When you first begin card-making, it's a little like being let loose in a sweet shop. There will be the tendency to do a trolley dash in every hobby store and craft fair. Many people tend to regret a lot of their early buys, as their experience grows and they develop their own style and preferences. Many people do, however, agree on the card-making basics, so this book highlights these along with some other card-making essentials.

Card making basics:

Adhesives: there's a mind-boggling array of adhesives on the market, but to start with your best bets are: double-sided tape, which can easily be trimmed to size; 3D foam tape or pads to add dimension; and a roller glue that is easy to dispense without making your fingers sticky.

Card: you can never have too much card! To give you flexibility in your designs, try making your own card blanks, as you can use just about any type and colour imaginable. A stash of white or cream card and envelopes are essential, and you will find 10 of each in this wallet.

Card stock: Available in every shade imaginable and in different weights (thicknesses) to suit, card stock is essential for matting, making your own card blanks, creating your own embellishments and much more.

Craft knife: there are many types of craft knives available and they prove indispensable when it comes to cutting and scoring. Invest in one that has a changeable blade, or choose a scalpel.

Cutting mat: you'll need two different types of cutting surface: a self-healing cutting mat for cutting, piercing and setting eyelets, and a PTFE-coated craft mat, preferably infused with glass for strength, non-stick and able to withstand high temperatures.

Decorative papers: there's much to be borrowed from scrapbooking, especially patterned paper, as so many are excellent for card backgrounds and offer good value for money, coming in 12x12" size.

Greetings: items such as rub-ons and peel-off greetings can be much maligned, but do serve a purpose, especially when you're stuck for a greeting in a hurry.

Heat gun: if you're going to be stamping and embossing, then this is an absolute essential. There are several designs to choose from, but it's a good idea to listen to other crafters' advice before you commit to a particular model.

Paper trimmer: essential for cutting pieces for layering and can help you to save money by cutting your own card blanks, as well as giving you the flexibility to make blanks from any sort of card to co-ordinate with your designs.

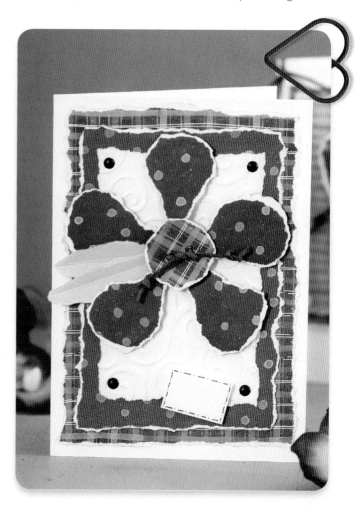

Scoring board and bone folder: a bone folder to give you a nice finish to the card folds and a scoring board to get the proportions correct.

Scissors: a large pair of kitchen scissors is fine for non-precision cutting, whereas you're likely to need a very small precision-tip pair for all the fiddly jobs that require pinpoint accuracy. You'll also be thankful for a pair of small Teflon-coated scissors to cut sticky materials with minimum hassle.

Things you might need:

Chalk inks: chalk inks are wonderful for creating backgrounds, just by sweeping across plain card. If you're not sure what you need, a number of inks are available in small sizes and can be the ideal low-cost choice for experimentation.

Dies: metal dies are incredibly useful for cutting paper, card stock and other materials into specific shapes. They come in a huge range of shapes and sizes, from simple squares and circles to ornate flowers and flourishes. While not an essential part of card-making they can make much neater end results and are very handy when producing cards in bulk.

Embossing powders: you can choose coloured embossing powder with a clear ink, or you can choose a coloured ink with clear embossing powder. For best results with fine images, detail is the perfect choice.

Greetings messages: it's worth considering background patterns and a few designs that you can use as main focal images. Messages such as 'Happy Birthday', 'With Love', 'Thinking of You' and similar non gender-based messages will get plenty of use. For background images, a text panel, music and a pattern such as a mesh can be the mainstay of your growing collection. Alphabets are wonderful for spelling out messages, and can also be multi-stamped as backgrounds. For main images the world is your oyster, but be careful what you choose: florals and leaves, for example, are always a safe bet and can be mixed and matched and used continually, each time with a different look.

Inkpads: a potential minefield, so where do you start? If you're going to be stamping in your card-making projects, one of life's absolute essentials is a good black inkpad: one that gives you excellent coverage and is versatile enough for different card surfaces.

Manual die-cutting machine: in order to use dies to cut different materials you will need to purchase a die-cutting machine. The material you want to cut and the die you are using are placed between two cutting plates and fed through the machine. It works like a mangle, putting the plates under pressure in order to cut the die design into your material.

Metal ruler: for cutting precision, particularly on shorter pieces and fiddly bits, this will accompany your craft knife or scalpel. You should avoid using wooden rulers.

Off-the-shelf embellishments: very handy to have at hand for quick card-making. There's plenty on offer to choose from, so you're sure to find what you need.

Pigment inks: generally, these are what you need if you're going to emboss, as they are slower drying than dye inks and allow you time to emboss.

Punches: hand punches are a cost-effective way of adding decorative main elements, as well as for corner and border decoration.

Rubber stamps: a stamper will probably argue that every rubberstamp in their collection is an essential item, but that's not exactly true! To avoid buying anything that simply looks nice, think about the types of cards that you're planning on making and consider the stamp designs that will be most useful to you.

Birthdays and Occasion

Pretty Cupcake

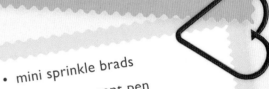

Your step-by-step guide:

1 Cover the middle of the card blank with black and pink swirl-patterned paper and tie a length of ribbon around the card.

2 Print a cupcake image onto white card stock and cut out. Add a doodled border with a black fineliner pen, and trim into a rectangle shape. Mount onto green patterned paper with foam pads and stick to the card.

3 Create little embellishments from white shrink plastic using a scalloped punch. Add doodled details and make a hole in the centre of each one with an eyelet tool. Shrink according to the manufacturer's instructions using a heat gun or oven.

4 Attach each shrunk embellishment with a mini sprinkle brad as shown.

Three Windows

Your step-by-step guide:

1 Crease-fold white card stock to create a 15x10 cm card blank. Attach pink card stock to the inside of the card, then cut out three apertures from the front, the middle aperture measuring 50x35 mm and the two smaller apertures measuring 35x35 mm.

2 Punch two circles and handcut a rectangle from green card stock. Draw dashes around each to create a border, then attach to the inside of the card behind the windows.

3 Stick acetate over the apertures, securing it inside the card. Stamp the bird and leaf images onto the acetate using permanent ink and colour using permanent pens.

4 Use the permanent pens to draw dashes around the windows, then complete the card by stamping or hand-writing the sentiment centrally.

You will need

- white card stock
- green and pink card stock
- acetate
- permanent coloured pens
- medium circle punch
- black inkpad
- bird stamp

Pretty Butterflies

Your step-by-step guide:

1 Cut the background panel from the sheet of patterned paper and attach centrally to your card blank.

2 Remove all the internal background from the dragonfly peel-off images, using the tip of your craft knife to lift them.

3 Attach the dragonflies to orange paper and cut around them, starting at the base of the tail for ease and making sure you angle your scissors for undercutting.

4 Glue the dragonflies to your card blank using 3D foam pads to lift the wing tips. Repeat the process with duplicate images to create the pink wing layers then finish with a nailhead in the centre of each dragonfly.

You will need

- square card blank
- patterned papers
- dragonfly peel-offs
- nailheads
- 3D foam pads
- scissors
- craft knife

Stitched Up

Your step-by-step guide:

1 Trace and cut a flower from white felt.

2 Stitch around the inside of the flower using pink embroidery thread in a running stitch.

3 Draw a circle onto pink felt and cut it out. Cut a smaller circle from green felt and stick to the pink circle using double-sided tape.

4 Add a row of blanket stitch around the outside of the green circle.

5 Sew a green button to the centre of the circle and attach to the middle of the white flower.

6 Assemble layers of white felt and pink card stock onto a dark green card blank before adding the white flower.

You will need

- white, pink and green felt
- embroidery thread
- needle
- button
- scissors
- double-sided tape
- green card blank

Monster Birthday

Your step-by-step guide:

1. Sew twice around the edge of the card face using a straight stitch in orange thread.

2. To make the monster truck, punch one red 1¾" circle and cut in half. Cut one half into quarters. Attach one quarter underneath the half circle so you have a straight edge along the bottom of the truck. Adhere two black 1" circles and two silver ¼" circles together and attach as wheels to the monster truck. Position the complete truck on the card using 3D foam pads.

3. To make the cars, punch ⅞" circles in blue and green card stock and cut in half. Punch ½" circles from the same colours and cut these in half too. Stick a smaller half under each larger semicircle. Punch the black wheels using a ¼" circle punch and attach to the bottom of each car. Position the three cars in a row along the base of the card using double-sided tape.

4. Punch three yellow ½" circles and stick to a 6x1.5 cm strip of black card stock to form a traffic light. Attach to the top right of the card.

5. Write or stamp your greeting along the top of the card above the monster truck.

You will need

- white card blank
- blue, yellow, red, black, silver and green card stock
- orange thread
- black pen
- ¼", ½", ⅞", 1" and 1¾" circle punches
- sewing machine
- 3D foam pads

Birthday Hugs

Your step-by-step guide:

1 Stamp the footballer image and colour with watercolour pencils remembering to add muddy patches. Stamp and colour the trophy, then trim around both.

2 Use a circular template to draw a 75 mm circle on the back of red gingham paper. Cut out and attach to the centre of a 12.5×12.5 cm card blank.

3 Draw zigzag faux stitching around the edges of the circle and stamp the greeting underneath.

4 Finish by attaching the footballer and trophy images to the circle using 3D foam pads.

You will need

- footballer and trophy stamp sets
- white card stock
- red gingham paper
- watercolour pencils and waterbrush
- black fineline pen
- black inkpad
- 3D foam pads

Woodpecker

Your step-by-step guide:

1 Trim a piece of card to create your 8" square card blank.

2 Mount the woodpecker image onto white card then mount onto green card, trimming to leave a wide border.

3 Cut all the elements out of the remaining découpage sheets, and assemble onto the base image using gel glue.

4 Trim the patterned backing paper, mount onto green card stock and trim to leave a narrow border, then attach to the base card.

5 Mount the woodpecker panel in the centre of the card using 3D foam tape, then wrap a piece of red organza ribbon around the spine to finish.

You will need

- various coloured card stock
- double-sided tape
- foam tape
- gel glue
- red organza ribbon
- patterned paper
- woodpecker image

Power Sphere

You will need

- copper, silver, dark green pearlescent card stock
- black, white and brown inkpads
- ink blending foam pads
- glue pen

- copper leaf
- woodware silver screw brads
- manual die-cutting machine
- Circle dies
- 1.8 cm, 2.5 cm circle punches
- template

Your step-by-step guide:

1   Create a 20x8 cm card blank from white card stock.

2   Using the template, cut the cylindrical part of the machine from green card stock, and the base, rings and sphere band from silver card stock. Ink the edges using a black inkpad, then use a blending pad to add white highlights down the cylinder.

3   Use a 2.5 cm circle die to cut the sphere from copper card stock, then ink the edges using a brown inkpad.

4   Attach the sphere to the card blank and trim the overlapping edge. Attach the dark green cylinder shape, the silver base and rings. Trim the card blank to fit, as shown.

5   Draw a bolt of lightning onto the sphere band using a glue pen. Allow to dry slightly before adding copper leaf. Once dry, gently brush away any excess copper leaf.

6   Punch two circles from coloured card stock and fix together with a screw brad. Attach to the sphere band to finish.

Cheers!

Your step-by-step guide:

1 Cover a 12.5 cm-square card blank with patterned paper. Matt a 3.5 cm strip of striped paper with dark brown paper, and trim to leave a narrow border. Attach across the centre of the card.

2 Stamp your digi image onto white card stock, colour using watercolour pencils and die-cut into a circle.

3 Layer the image circle onto a 10 cm square of polka dot-patterned paper and attach to the centre of the card using 3D foam pads.

4 Decorate the corners of the polka dot square using aqua rainbow drops to finish.

You will need

- patterned papers
- digi stamps
- chalk ink
- rainbow drops
- watercolour pencils
- white card stock
- circle dies

Gone Fishing

Your step-by-step guide:

1. Trim a piece of patterned paper to fit the front of a 14.5 cm square card blank, leaving a narrow border around the edges.

2. Cut a 9.5x11.5 cm piece of polka-dot patterned paper and stick towards the left-hand side of the card. Decorate with a strip of co-ordinating patterned paper as shown.

3. Stamp your digi image onto white card stock, colour using watercolour pencils and trim into a rectangle. Matt with cream patterned paper and ink the edges. Add two patterned paper tabs to the lower right-hand corner of the panel and decorate with card candy.

4. Attach the finished image panel to the centre of the card using 3D foam pads.

You will need

- patterned paper
- digi stamps
- card candy
- watercolour pencils
- white card stock
- chalk ink

Floral Fan

Your step-by-step guide:

1 Take four yellow and three pink flowers and twist the stems together. Wrap the flowers and fans together using organza ribbon.

2 Cover the card front with patterned paper, then add a 3.5x14.5 cm strip of navy card stock to the righthand side and add a piece of organza ribbon on top.

3 Cut the stem off one of the flowers and twist round the outside of the organza ribbon, leaving excess at the back of the bunch, then carefully pierce a hole approximately a third of the way up the card front. Thread the excess stem through and secure using double-sided tape.

Pretty Beads

Your step-by-step guide:

1 Sponge one ink of your choice onto one side of a domino-sized piece of stampboard and a different coloured ink onto the other side. Stamp over the piece with a texture block using your first choice of ink.

2 Let the whole thing dry completely, then pat the inkpad over the surface. Cover with enamel and heat to melt. Repeat three times to build up a thick layer of enamel.

3 Fix a ball of sticky-tack onto the underside of the piece and use it to steady the surface of the stampboard while you add gold dry glitter around the edge of the stampboard and on the circles on the design, then leave to dry.

4 Cut a small piece of beaded trim and fix it to the back of the stampboard using tape. Attach the pin fastener.

5 Assemble the flower elements together and stick to the front of the stampboard.

You will need

- stampboard
- a variety of inkpads
- watermark inkpad
- embossing enamel

- gold glitter glue
- craft flowers
- small rosebud
- beaded trim
- sticky tack
- stamp set
- self-adhesive pin back

Wedding Wishes

You will need

- groom and bride images
- white card stock
- silver mirri card
- gemstones
- white ribbon

- scalloped and straight rectangles & scalloped and straight oval dies
- embossing folder
- die-cutting machine
- pc & printer
- foam pads

Your step-by-step guide:

1 Create a 10x21 cm card blank from white card stock.

2 Cut a heart shape from silver mirri card and stick to the front of the card.

3 Cut a piece of white ribbon to measure approximately 20 cm long and glue the dress stand to the centre, then affix to the card front.

4 Emboss the dress and groom, adhere both and decorate with gemstones.

5 Cut the ends of the ribbon to form a fringed effect, fold to form a shoulder wrap effect and glue down. Add gems to finish.

Silver Heart Wedding

Your step-by-step guide:

1. Stamp the bride & groom image onto white card stock. Allow to dry, then colour using marker pens and trim.

2. Die-cut a large heart from silver card stock, and mount the bride & groom onto the heart using 3D foam pads. Punch tiny hearts from mid-blue card stock and attach, then decorate the bride with pearls.

3. Cut a piece of navy card stock to 11x12.5 cm and round the corners. Stick a strip of 10x12 cm patterned paper across the panel, then mount the silver heart in the centre.

4. Trim a 7 cm-wide section from the front panel of the card and round the edges. Attach the image panel as shown, affixing only on the left-hand side.

5. Tie ribbon into a knot around the left-hand side of the card and add glitter glue highlights to finish.

You will need

- black inkpad
- marker pens
- white 14.5 cm-square card blank
- white, mid-blue, royal blue and silver card stock
- flat-backed pearls

- white sheer polka dot ribbon
- glitter glue
- corner-rounder punch
- heart border punch
- heart die
- various patterned papers
- wedding stamps

Tiny Toes

Your step-by-step guide:

1. Create a 4" square card blank from pink card stock. Cover the bottom half of the card with patterned paper.

2. Draw an 'X' in the centre of the card front, with the outermost points where you want the corners of your opening to be. Cut along these lines with a craft knife to give four triangular flaps. Rip these triangles out, curling and scuffing the edges as you go.

3. Glue a piece of ribbon across the front of the card, over the paper join and across the aperture. Tie the tag around the top of the card with the same ribbon, and finish with a crystal gem.

You will need

- patterned card stock
- paper
- a variety of ribbons
- chipboard tag
- crystal gem
- craft knife

Bouncy Baby

Your step-by-step guide:

1 Colour in your rabbit die-cut and highlight with glitter glue. Set aside to dry, before attaching to the card front.

2 Stamp the letters onto the foampad using a permanent inkpad. Attach to the card front using foam pad.

3 Wrap ribbon around the card front and tie to secure.

You will need

- 96 mm-square scalloped card blank
- rabbit die-cut
- 3D foam pads
- ribbon
- glitter glue
- alphabet stamps
- permanent black inkpad

Seasonal

The Gift of Christmas

Your step-by-step guide:

1 Cut a square of mid-blue card stock to fit the card front, distress the edges, then attach.

2 Print out the green snowflake paper, then distress and ink the edges. Matt with green card stock, distress the edges again and fix to the centre of the card.

3 Stamp the gift stack onto white card stock, and colour using watercolour crayons and a waterbrush. Trim to measure 7.5x5.5 cm, then distress and ink the edges.

4 Cut an oblong of blue card stock to measure 8x6 cm and an oblong of green card stock to 9x7 cm. Round the corners and distress the edges, then layer and attach to the card. Mount the stamped image on top using 3D foam pads.

4 Tie polka dot ribbon around the spine of the card and knot at the front. Highlight with glitter glue and add three self-adhesive pearls to the bottom-right corner.

You will need

- stamp pad foam
- white 5" square card blank
- white card stock
- corner-rounder punch
- black inkpad
- polka dot ribbon

- glitter glue
- green and red self-adhesive pearls
- water colour crayons
- blue and green card stock
- distressing tool
- distress inkpad

Starbright

Your step-by-step guide:

1 Create four white clay stars by applying a cutter to a sheet of white modelling clay. Bake the clay following the manufacturer's instructions and allow it to cool.

2 Layer the card blank with panels of green, red and white paper.

3 Cut a 10 cm-tall triangular tree from a piece of green card stock and a narrow 4 cm pot from red card stock.

4 Insert brads at equal intervals to the inner edges of the tree and fix both the tree and the pot to the card using 3D foam pads.

5 Attach the clay stars to the card.

You will need

- white modelling clay
- white A6 card blank
- star cutter set
- green, red and white paper and card stock
- tiny green and red brads
- non-stick roller, PVA glue, sticky foam pads
- baking surface and domestic oven

Christmas Trees

Your step-by-step guide:

1 Cut out three triangles (4 cm wide and 6 cm tall) from the lime green card stock. Attach strips of double-sided tape diagonally across each. Remove the backing from the tape and sprinkle with gold glitter. Tap off the excess.

2 Cut a 13x8.5 cm piece of pale yellow card stock. Punch three stars from yellow card stock, and mount onto the pale yellow panel along with the three trees, using foam pads. Add rhinestones.

3 Matt your tree panel with lime green card stock leaving a narrow border.

4 Fold an A5 piece of yellow card stock in half to form your card blank. Apply a strip of glitter across the middle using the same technique as above, then affix the tree panel onto the front.

You will need

- star punch
- red, green and yellow 4 mm self-adhesive rhinestones
- gold ultra-fine glitter
- pale yellow, golden yellow and lime green card stock
- 6 mm double-sided tape
- double-sided foam tape

Snowy Day

Your step-by-step guide:

1. Crease-fold white card stock to create a 15 cm square card blank. Trim scroll paper to fit and matt with purple then silver card stock. Wrap with lilac ribbon and attach to the card front.

2. Stamp your chosen image with black ink. Colour with a variety of markers and then sprinkle with ultra thick embossing powder. Heat with a heat gun.

3. Once the embossing powder has melted, repeat this step twice more. Allow to cool, then cut into a circle shape and matt with purple card stock.

4. Use a die cutting machine and snowflake die to cut a snowflake from white glitter card and attach to the top of the card front, overlapping the ribbon.

5. Mount your embossed image in the centre of the card, slightly overlapping the snowflake. Make a bow from a small piece of lilac ribbon and stick to the top of the image.

6. Punch three small snowflakes from purple and silver card stock and white glitter card using a snowflake punch. Affix in the bottom-right of the card, fixing silver stones to the centre of each to finish.

You will need

- an image of your choice
- white, silver and purple card stock
- scroll paper
- snowflake stamp
- lilac ribbon

- silver gemstones
- black inkpad
- watermark inkpad
- embossing powder
- heat gun
- embossing machine
- snowflake die
- snowflake punch

Christmas Tag

Your step-by-step guide:

1. Cut two patterned paper matts to fit the card front and attach together. Stamp snowflakes in the top-left and bottom-right corners and heat-emboss.

2. Cut a tag shape from card stock, emboss using the embossing folder, distress the edges then matt onto a slightly larger patterned paper tag.

3. Set an eyelet in the top of the tag, thread ribbon through then secure to the card front at an angle using silicone glue.

4. Die-cut the village image from patterned paper and, with the die-cut still in the die, brush water mark over the rooftops. Remove the die-cut from the die, sprinkle with embossing powder and heat.

5. Place the die-cut back into the die and brush turquoise ink over the tree. Remove the die-cut, edge with sepia ink then attach to the tag using 3D foam pads. Add glitter glue to the edges of the tag to finish.

You will need

- cream 10.5x14.8 cm card blank
- patterned paper
- card stock
- snowflakes stamps
- white embossing powder
- watermark inkpad
- heat tool

- embossing folder
- die-cutting machine
- turquoise and sepia inkpads
- squeeze tool
- glitter glue
- eyelet
- sheer ribbon
- silicone glue and 3D foam pads

Easter Eggs

Your step-by-step guide:

1. Cut 2" from the open side of your card blank so that it now measures 3x7". Ink the edges using green fluid chalk.

2. Using one of the offcuts, cut 1" from the top. Ink the edges in green fluid chalk, then matt onto the pink patterned paper. Crop to form a ½" border all round. Matt centrally onto the card blank using 3D foam pads.

3. Choose four of the decorated eggs from the sticker sheet and fix onto the panel, adhering the first and third eggs with foam pads to raise them from the card.

4. As a finishing touch and to add some bling, fix an adhesive gem to the centre of the second and fourth eggs.

You will need

- easter sticker sheet
- craft essentials kit
- white 5x7" card blank
- green fluid chalk inkpad
- double-sided tape
- 3D foam pads

Pretty Circles

Your step-by-step guide:

1 Make an A6-sized side-fold card blank from card stock, and trim 1 cm off the front righthand edge. Punch four 1½" circles from the patterned papers and attach down the right-hand side of the card, making sure you line them up with the back edge.

2 Punch a 3" circle from green card stock and a 2½" circle from cream card stock. Stamp and emboss your image onto the smaller circle and colour with water colour. Layer the circles together and attach to the card base using 3D foam pads.

3 Cut out a small daisy from the patterned paper, attach to the card, and add candy buttons down the right-hand side of the card and in the centre of the flower.

You will need

- 1½", 3" and 2½" circle punches
- daisy shapecut
- watercolour set
- variety of patterned papers
- varity of card stock
- candy buttons
- image stamp

Easter Bonnet

Your step-by-step guide:

1 Make a 14.4 cm-square tent-fold card blank from card stock.

2 Trim a piece of patterned paper to 14.4x7.5 cm and attach across the bottom of the card. Cover the join with a craft frill.

3 Cut card stock to 9 cm square, and tape ribbon tabs to the top right-hand edge.

4 Stamp and emboss your image onto an 8.5 cm square of card stock, and colour using watercolour set. Attach to the panel. Attach the panel to the centre of the card, then add candy buttons.

You will need

- watercolour set
- striped paper
- craft frill
- variety of card stock
- yellow ribbon
- candy buttons

Hey Chick!

Your step-by-step guide:

1. Make a 14.4 cm-square side-fold card blank from cream card stock.

2. Trim the patterned papers to measure 12x12.5 cm. Hold together with a paper clip whilst you cut a wavy edge along the top, then cut into three 4 cm strips. Matt with green card stock, leaving a narrow border, and trim to follow the curve along the top. Attach to the centre of the card.

3. Cut a strip of green card stock and stick to the righthand side of the card, then fix two buttons to the right-hand edge.

3. Stamp and emboss your image onto a 7x5 cm piece of cream card stock, then colour using watercolour set. Matt with green card stock, leaving a narrow border around the edges and attach to the card using 3D foam pads.

You will need
- watercolour set
- patterned papers
- cream and green card stock
- pastel buttons

Wooden Heart

Your step-by-step guide:

1 Trim a piece of kraft card stock to measure 21×10.5 cm and creasefold to create a card blank.

2 Stamp stripes in black horizontally and vertically across the front of the card to create a chequered pattern. Ink the edges of the card using a black inkpad.

3 Trim a piece of kraft card to measure 4.5 cm square and emboss using the embossing folder.

4 Emboss a piece of green card stock with the small square folder and ink the edges with black ink.

5 Colour the wooden heart using a red inkpad and assemble the card.

You will need

- kraft card stock
- stripes stamp
- wooden heart
- red and black inkpads
- shape cutting embossing machine
- small square folders

Heart of Hearts

Your step-by-step guide:

1 Stamp five hearts onto white card stock, one in red, one in pink, two in black and one in grey ink.

2 Cut out all of the stamped hearts and affix to the card front using silicone glue.

You will need

- white A6 card blank
- white card stock
- heart stamps
- pink and red inkpad
- grey inkpad
- black inkpad
- silicone glue

Best Wishes

Get Well Soon

Your step-by-step guide:

1. Follow the guide on the right to create the coloured dragon image. Apply gloss medium to his toenails and spine.

2. Cut a 10.5 cm wide strip from the length of the A4 card stock and score across the piece at 10.5 cm, 21 cm and 25.3 cm. Fold along the score lines to create your two-layer card blank.

3. Attach a piece of dotty paper to the front layer and pink floral paper to the second layer, leaving narrow borders.

4. Cut a tag shape from pink paper and stamp or write your greeting onto it. Layer onto a slightly larger piece of green paper, aligning the left-hand edges, then punch two small holes through both layers.

5. Tie a length of ribbon through the holes and finish with a ribbon bow, then attach the tag and the stamped image to your card front using 3D foam pads.

Colour a stamped image step-by-step

1. Swipe your card stock with an anti-static bag then stamp your image using an embossing ink; sprinkle the embossing powder over and tip away the excess. Heat the image until the powder is melted and shiny, then cut around the image leaving a border.

2. Spritz your paint pots with water then apply a watered-down base coat to all the main areas of the image – for shading, always work in one direction so that the lighter areas have the paint applied last, as it will be less intense.

3. Add fresh layers of diluted paint to any areas you want to be darker and use the paint less diluted on areas you want saturated with colour.

44

You will need

- selection of card stock
- watercolour paints
- cartoon of your choice
- embossing inkpad
- embossing powder
- anti-static magic bag

- patterned paper
- gloss medium
- pink organza ribbon
- heat gun
- scoreboard & bone folder
- hole punch
- 3D foam pads

Doily Vase

Your step-by-step guide:

1 Emboss a sheet of patterned paper using an embossing folder. Match up the embossed pattern on the remaining paper and run through the machine again.

2 Create a background paper by stamping within the diamonds using the stamp with green ink, the leaf stamp with dark green and the ribbon swirl with blue. Ink the stamp each time, before stamping. When dry, cut out the embossed and patterned part of the paper and affix to the front of a white 14 cm-square card blank. Because of the size of the embossing folder, it will fall short of the card spine, so use the doily punch to punch an edge in a contrasting patterned paper (save the waste strip), then in the same paper to cover the space. Finish with the waste strip from the contrasting paper.

3 Die-cut a circle from smooth white card stock and stamp the vase stamp using blue ink. Add in and ink. Rotate the stamps and stamp at least twice before reinking. Add sprig stamp in dark green ink and leaf stamp in green, turning the placement line towards the flowers. Add ribbon swirl stamp in blue ink.

4 Ink the edges of the circle using yellow chalk or ink, then matt onto a scalloped circle die-cut from patterned paper then onto a doily. Affix to the card front.

5 Die-cut two dragonflies from cream card stock and attach to the card front using 3D foam pads. Decorate with yellow pearls and glitter glue to finish.

You will need

- white 14 cm square blank card
- white and cream card stock
- patterned paper
- flower rubber stamp
- yellow pearls
- various coloured inkpads
- flower, sprig, leaf and vase rubber stamps

- yellow chalk
- doily punch
- embossing folder
- dragonfly cutting die
- die cutting machine
- circle die cutter
- 3D foam pads
- glitter glue